图书在版编目（CIP）数据

霍顿听见了呼呼的声音/(美)苏斯著；李育超译–北京：中国对外翻译出版公司，2007.1
（苏斯博士双语经典）书名原文：Horton Hears a Who
ISBN 978-7-5001-1714-8

I.霍… II. ①苏…②李… III. ①英语–汉语–对照读物②童话–美国–现代 IV. H319.4:I

中国版本图书馆 CIP 数据核字(2006)第 142731 号

（著作权合同登记：图字 01-2006-7168 号）

出版发行 / 中国对外翻译出版公司
地　　址 / 北京市西城区车公庄大街甲 4 号物华大厦六层
电　　话 / (010)68359376　68359303　68359101　68357937
邮　　编 / 100044
传　　真 / (010)68357870
电子邮箱 / book@ctpc.com.cn
网　　址 / http://www.ctpc.com.cn

策划编辑 / 李育超　薛振冰　王晓颖
责任编辑 / 薛振冰
特约编辑 / 王　甘
责任校对 / 韩建荣　卓　玛
英文朗读 / Rayna Martinez & Camila Tamayo
封面设计 / 大象设计

排　　版 / 翰文阳光
印　　刷 / 北京画中画印刷有限公司
经　　销 / 新华书店

规　　格 / 787×1092毫米　1/16
印　　张 / 4.5
字　　数 / 20 千字
版　　次 / 2007 年 4 月第一版
印　　次 / 2013 年 5 月第六次

ISBN 978-7-5001-1714-8　定价：18.60 元

音频下载：登录 http://www.ctpc.com.cn 点击"苏斯博士双语经典"。

　　本书采用了隐形码点读技术，页码所在的椭圆部分置入了隐形码，可配合爱国者点读笔产品点读发音。

HORTON HEARS A WHO!

霍顿听见了呼呼的声音

［美］Dr. Seuss 图文

苗卉 译

中国出版集团
中国对外翻译出版公司

Think left and think right and think low and think high.
Oh, the things you can think up if only you try!

左想想，右想想，上面想想，下面想想。哦，只要你去
尝试，你就能想出好多好多东西。

——苏斯博士

★二十世纪最卓越的儿童文学作家之一
★一生创作48种精彩绘本
★作品被翻译成20多种文字和盲文
★全球销量逾2.5亿册
★曾获得美国图画书最高荣誉凯迪克
　大奖和普利策特殊贡献奖
★两次获奥斯卡金像奖和艾美奖
★美国教育部指定的重要阅读辅导读物

苏斯是谁？

虽然苏斯博士创造了许多妙趣横生的动物形象，但他一直不愿意将自己的作品改编成图书以外的形式，因此，以苏斯作品为蓝本的影视作品屈指可数。

1966 年，苏斯授权声名显赫的动画艺术家查克·琼斯将《圣诞怪杰》拍成了动画片，这部影片非常忠实于原作，至今仍被许多人认为是一部经典之作，并被列入每年的圣诞特别节目。随后被搬上银幕的还有《霍顿听见了呼呼的声音》、《绒毛树》和《戴高帽子的猫》等。

晚年时期，苏斯博士似乎通融了一些，因而又有一些以苏斯创造的动物形象为模型的卡通片和玩具应运而生。1991 年苏斯博士去世后，他的遗孀开始负责所有的授权事宜。2000 年由她批准上演了金·凯瑞主演的《圣诞怪杰》和百老汇音乐剧《苏斯狂想曲》，2003 年又上演了麦克·迈尔斯主演的《戴高帽子的猫》。

好莱坞新老喜剧明星金·凯瑞和史蒂夫·卡洛尔将在根据苏斯博士同名原著改编的动画片《霍顿听见了呼呼的声音》中合作，金·凯瑞将为大象霍顿配音，卡洛尔为呼呼镇镇长配音。这也是两位喜剧天王的首次合作。

For My Great Friend,
Mitsugi Nakamura
of Kyoto,
Japan.

谨以此书献给我的好朋友，
日本京都的中村端希。

On the fifteenth of May,
In the Jungle of Nool,
In the heat of the day,
In the cool of the pool,
He was splashing . . . enjoying the jungle's great joys . . .
When Horton the elephant heard a small noise.

五月十五日,在努尔丛林里一天中最炎热的时候,大象霍顿在凉爽的池塘中拍打着水花,尽情享受丛林的欢乐。这时,他听到了一个微小的声音。

So Horton stopped splashing. He looked toward the sound.
"That's funny," thought Horton. "There's no one around."
Then he heard it again! Just a very faint yelp
As if some tiny person were calling for help.
"I'll help you," said Horton. "But *who* are you? *Where?*"
He looked and he looked. He could see nothing there
But a small speck of dust blowing past through the air.

　　于是,霍顿停了下来,向发出声音的方向张望。"真奇怪,"霍顿想,"周围一
个人都没有。"可接着,他又听到了那个声音,是一声非常微弱的叫喊,好像一些
小人儿在求助。"我会帮助你的,"霍顿说,"可是,你是谁?你在哪里啊?"他看了
又看,什么也没发现,只有一个小灰尘粒从空中飘过。

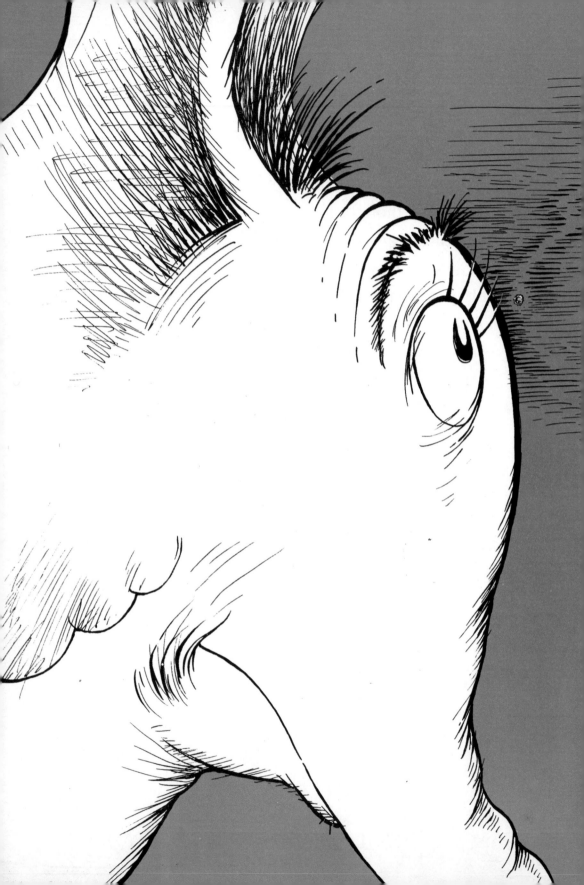

"I say!" murmured Horton. "I've never heard tell
Of a small speck of dust that is able to yell.
So you know what I think? . . . Why, I think that there must
Be someone on top of that small speck of dust!
Some sort of a creature of *very* small size,
Too small to be seen by an elephant's eyes . . .

"哎呀！"霍顿低声嘟囔着，"我从没听说过小灰尘粒也会说话。你
知道我是怎么想的吗？我想肯定是有人在小灰尘粒顶上！有些家伙
非常非常小，小到大象的眼睛看不到。"

"… some poor little person who's shaking with fear
That he'll blow in the pool! He has no way to steer!
I'll just have to save him. Because, after all,
A person's a person, no matter how small."

　　"有个可怜的小人儿在发抖，他害怕自己被吹到池塘里！他无法控制自己的方向！我得去救他。因为，一个人不管多么微小也是个人。"

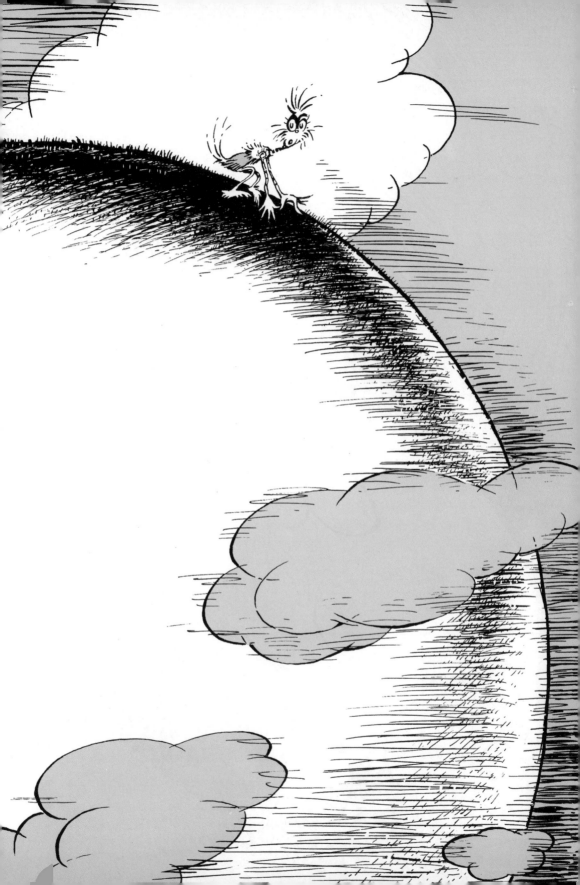

So, gently, and using the greatest of care,
The elephant stretched his great trunk through the air,
And he lifted the dust speck and carried it over
And placed it down, safe, on a very soft clover.

于是,大象小心翼翼地伸出大鼻子,轻轻举起灰尘粒,稳稳地把它放在一株很柔软的苜蓿上。

"Humpf!" humpfed a voice. 'Twas a sour kangaroo.
And the young kangaroo in her pouch said "Humpf!" too.
"Why, that speck is as small as the head of a pin.
A person on *that*? ...Why, there never has been!"

"哼!"一只袋鼠酸溜溜地哼了一声,她袋子里的小袋鼠也跟着哼了一声。"什么?针鼻儿大的灰尘,还能有人在上面?哎呀,根本不可能!"

"Believe me," said Horton. "I tell you sincerely,
My ears are quite keen and I heard him quite clearly.
I *know* there's a person down there. And, what's more,
Quite likely there's two. Even three. Even four.
Quite likely . . .

" . . . a family, for all that we know!
A family with children just starting to grow.
So, please," Horton said, "as a favor to me,
Try not to disturb them. Just please let them be."

　　"相信我,"霍顿说,"是真的,我的耳朵很敏锐,可以听得清清楚楚。我
知道有个人在那儿,而且,很可能是两个,甚至三个、四个,很可能……

　　"……有一个家庭,像我们都知道的那样!一个有孩子正在成长的家
庭。"霍顿说,"所以,看在我的份儿上,请不要打扰他们,就让他们那样安
安稳稳呆着吧。"

"I think you're a fool!" laughed the sour kangaroo
And the young kangaroo in her pouch said, "Me, too!
You're the biggest blame fool in the Jungle of Nool!"
And the kangaroos plunged in the cool of the pool.
"What terrible splashing!" the elephant frowned.
"I can't let my very small persons get drowned!
I've *got* to protect them. I'm bigger than they."
So he plucked up the clover and hustled away.

　　"我看你真是个笨蛋!"袋鼠阴阳怪气地笑了起来,她袋子里的小袋
鼠附和着说:"我也这么认为。你是努尔丛林里最大的笨蛋!"袋鼠跳进
了清凉的池塘里。"多可怕的水花啊!"大象皱起了眉头,"我可不能让我
的小人儿淹死。我要保护他们。我比他们大。"他摘下苜蓿,匆匆跑开了。

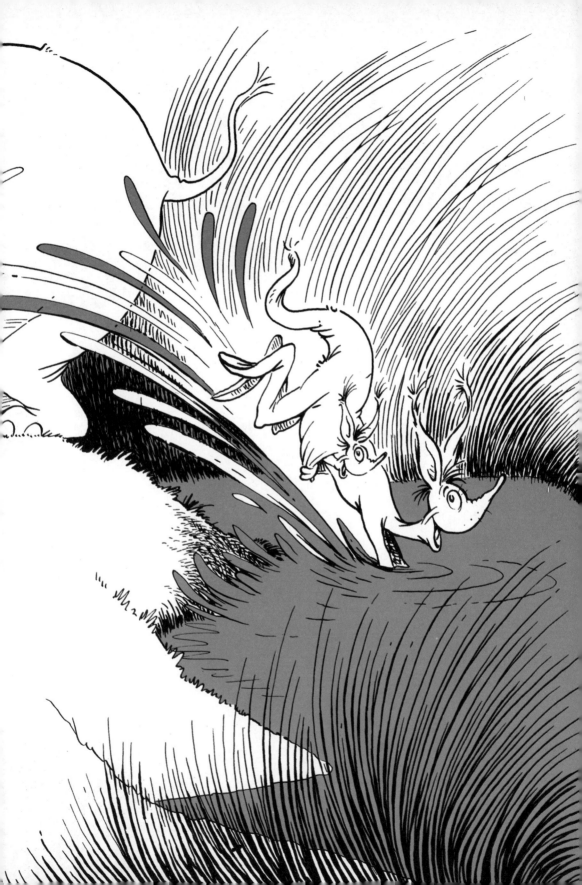

Through the high jungle tree tops, the news quickly spread:
"He talks to a dust speck! He's out of his head!
Just look at him walk with that speck on that flower!"
And Horton walked, worrying, almost an hour.
"Should I put this speck down?..." Horton thought with alarm.
"If I do, these small persons may come to great harm.
I *can't* put it down. And I *won't!* After all
A person's a person. No matter how small."

通过丛林高高的树顶,霍顿的事儿飞快传开了:"他居然对一个灰尘粒说话。他真是晕了头了。快看,他把灰尘粒放在小花上,还托着走呢!"霍顿走了都快一个小时了,他忧心忡忡。"我该把这个小灰尘粒放下来吗?"霍顿忐忑不安地想,"如果我这么做了,这些小人儿可能会受到巨大的伤害。我不能把它丢下。我不会的!毕竟,每个人都是一个生命,不管他有多么小。"

Then Horton stopped walking.

The speck-voice was talking!

The voice was so faint he could just barely hear it.

"Speak *up*, please," said Horton, He put his ear near it.

"My friend," came the voice, "you're a *very* fine friend.

You've helped all us folks on this dust speck no end.

You've saved all our houses, our ceilings and floors.

You've saved all our churches and grocery stores."

　　接着,霍顿停下了脚步。那个小灰尘粒开口说话了!可声音非常微弱,霍顿几乎听不到。"请大声点儿。"霍顿说。他把耳朵贴了上去。

　　"我的朋友,"声音传了出来,"你是一个非常好的朋友。你帮了这粒灰尘上的所有人一个大忙!你保全了我们所有的房子、天花板和地板。你保全了我们所有的教堂和杂货店。"

"You mean. . ." Horton gasped, "you have *buildings* there, *too?*"
"Oh, yes," piped the voice. "We most certainly do. . . .
"I know," called the voice, "I'm too small to be seen
But I'm Mayor of a town that is friendly and clean.
Our buildings, to you, would seem terribly small
But to us, who aren't big, they are wonderfully tall.
My town is called *Who*-ville, for I am a *Who*
And we *Whos* are all thankful and grateful to you."
And Horton called back to the Mayor of the town,
"You're safe now. Don't worry. I won't let you down."

"你是说……"霍顿惊讶得喘不过气来,"你们那里也有房子?""哦,是的。"那个声音尖叫着说,"我们当然有……我知道,"那个声音喊道,"我太小,人们看不到,但是我是这个小镇的镇长,我们的小镇友好而整洁。对你们来说,我们的房子看起来太小了。但是对我们这些小人儿来说,它们高大而雄伟。我们的小镇叫呼呼镇,因为我是一个呼呼,我们呼呼都非常感激你。"霍顿对呼呼镇长说:"你现在安全了。别担心,我不会让你们失望的。"

But, just as he spoke to the Mayor of the speck,
Three big jungle monkeys climbed up Horton's neck!
The Wickersham Brothers came shouting "What rot!
This elephant's talking to *Whos* who are *not*!
There *aren't* any *Whos*! And they *don't* have a Mayor!
And *we're* going to stop all this nonsense! *So there!* "

　　但是，就在他与灰尘粒上的镇长交谈的时候，丛林里的三只大猴子——威克兄弟爬上了霍顿的脖子！他们大声喊道："真是荒唐！这头大象在跟不存在的东西说话！哪里有什么呼呼！还有什么镇长！我们不能让他们胡说八道！快！"

They snatched Horton's clover! They carried it off
To a black-bottomed eagle named Vlad Vlad-i-koff,
A mighty strong eagle, of very swift wing,
And they said, "Will you kindly get rid of this thing?"
And, before the poor elephant even could speak,
That eagle flew off with the flower in his beak.

他们抢走了霍顿的苜蓿!把它给了一只叫弗弗的黑尾巴鹰。那是一只
非常强健的老鹰,长着一对迅捷的大翅膀。猴子们对老鹰说:"请你行行好,
把这个东西丢掉吧?"可怜的大象还没来得及开口,老鹰就叼着苜蓿飞走了。

All that late afternoon and far into the night
That black-bottomed bird flapped his wings in fast flight,
While Horton chased after, with groans, over stones
That tattered his toenails and battered his bones,
And begged, "Please don't harm all my little folks, who
Have as much right to live as us bigger folks do!"

But far, far beyond him, that eagle kept flapping
And over his shoulder called back, "Quit your yapping.
I'll fly the night through. I'm a bird. I don't mind it.
And I'll hide this, tomorrow, where *you'll* never find it!"

从黄昏一直到黑夜,那只黑尾巴鹰拍打着翅膀一个劲儿地飞呀飞呀。霍顿就一直跟着他跑呀跑呀,痛苦极了。石头磨破了他的脚趾,刺疼了他的骨头,他请求道:"请不要伤害我的小伙伴们,他们和我们大人一样有权生存。"

但是,鹰还在不停地飞,他回头喊道:"别说啦!我能飞一整夜。我是一只鸟。我才不在乎呢。我明天会把它藏起来,让你永远也找不到。"

And at 6:56 the next morning he did it.
It sure was a terrible place that he hid it.
He let that small clover drop somewhere inside
Of a great patch of clovers a hundred miles wide!
"Find THAT!" sneered the bird. "But I think you will fail."
And he left
With a flip
Of his black-bottomed tail.

 第二天早上六点五十六分,他真的这样做了。他把它藏到了一个可怕的地方。他把小苜蓿扔到了一百英里见方的一大片苜蓿堆里!"去找吧!"鹰冷笑道,"你肯定找不到,哈哈。"他调转黑色的尾巴飞走了。

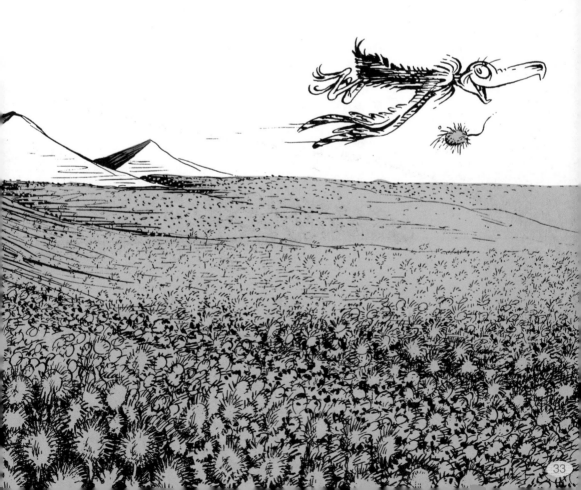

"I'll find it!" cried Horton. "I'll find it or bust!
I SHALL find my friends on my small speck of dust!"
And clover, by clover, by clover with care
He picked up and searched them, and called, "Are you there?"
But clover, by clover, by clover he found
That the one that he sought for was just not around.
And by noon poor old Horton, more dead than alive,
Had picked, searched, and piled up, nine thousand and five.

　　"我会找到它的!"霍顿喊道,"我就是粉身碎骨也要找到它。我一定能找到小小灰尘粒上的朋友们!"于是,他小心翼翼地拿起一株株苜蓿,不停地寻找,不停地问:"你们在那儿吗?"他一株苜蓿一株苜蓿地找呀找呀,但是并没有找到要找的那个。中午时分,可怜的老霍顿都快累死了。他把苜蓿捡起来,察看一番,再堆起来,足足重复了九千零五次。

Then, on through the afternoon, hour after hour . . .
Till he found them at last! On the three millionth flower!
"My friends!" cried the elephant. "Tell me! Do tell!
Are you safe? Are you sound? Are you whole? Are you well?"

　　下午继续找,一个小时又一个小时过去了……终于,他找到了他们!在第三百万
朵小花上!"我的朋友们!"大象哭了,"告诉我!快告诉我呀!你们安全吗?你们好吗?
你们完好无损吗?你们都好好的吗?"

From down on the speck came the voice of the Mayor:

"We've *really* had trouble! Much more than our share.

When that black-bottomed birdie let go and we dropped,

We landed so hard that our clocks have all stopped.

Our tea-pots are broken. Our rocking-chairs smashed.

And our bicycle tires all blew up when we crashed.

So, Horton, *please!*" pleaded that voice of the Mayor's,

"Will you stick by us *Whos* while we're making repairs?"

"Of course," Horton answered. "Of course I will stick.

I'll stick by you small folks through thin and through thick!"

灰尘粒里传来了镇长的声音:

"我们确实遇到了麻烦!远远超过了我们的承受能力。那只黑尾巴鹰把我们扔下来的时候,我们摔得太重了,所有的钟都停了,茶壶破了,摇椅碎了,自行车胎全爆了。所以,霍顿,求求你!"镇长请求道,"我们重整家园的时候,你能和呼呼镇的人们在一起吗?"

"当然,"霍顿回答,"我当然会,不管发生什么事,我都会始终和你们在一起。"

"Humpf!"

Humpfed a voice!

"For almost two days you've run wild and insisted

On chatting with persons who've never existed.

Such carryings-on in our peaceable jungle!

We've had quite enough of your bellowing bungle!

And I'm here to state," snapped the big kangaroo,

"That your silly nonsensical game is all through!"

And the young kangaroo in her pouch said, "Me, too!"

"哼!"一个声音哼了一声。"这两天你真是疯了,一个劲儿地对不存在的人说话。我们平静的丛林竟有这样失常的行为!我们受够了你的胡言乱语了!现在我宣布,"大袋鼠气冲冲地说,"你那愚蠢荒谬的游戏到此结束!"她袋子里的小袋鼠也随声附和:"到此结束!"

"With the help of the Wickersham Brothers and dozens
Of Wickersham Uncles and Wickersham Cousins
And Wickersham In-Laws, whose help I've engaged,
You're going to be roped! And you're going to be caged!
And, as for your dust speck . . . hah! *That* we shall boil
In a hot steaming kettle of Beezle-Nut oil!"

"*Boil* it? . . ." gasped Horton!
"Oh, that you *can't* do!
It's all full of persons!
They'll *prove* it to you!"

"我已经联合了威克兄弟以及众多的威克叔
伯、兄弟姐妹和亲戚朋友们,我们要用绳子把你捆
起来,关到笼子里去!至于你的灰尘粒嘛,哈哈!我
们会把它扔到滋滋冒着热气的坚果油壶里煮!"

"煮?"霍顿大吃一惊,"哦,你不能那么做!那里
面都是人!他们会证明给你看的!"

"Mr. Mayor! Mr. Mayor!" Horton called. "Mr. Mayor!
You've *got* to prove now that you really are there!
So call a big meeting. Get everyone out.
Make every *Who* holler! Make every *Who* shout!
Make every *Who* scream! If you don't, every *Who*
Is going to end up in a Beezle-Nut stew!"

　　"镇长先生!镇长先生!"霍顿喊了起来,"镇长先生,现在你必须证明你
们真的在那里!赶紧开个大会,让大家都出来。让每个呼呼都叫起来,喊起
来!让每个呼呼都大声叫嚷!不然,每个呼呼都会在滋滋冒着热气的坚果炖
汤中结束生命。"

And, down on the dust speck, the scared little Mayor
Quick called a big meeting in *Who*-ville Town Square.
And his people cried loudly. They cried out in fear:
"We are here! We are here! We are here! We are here!"

灰尘粒里，惊恐不安的小镇长很快在呼呼镇的中心广场召开了一个大
会。他的市民大声呼叫，他们胆战心惊地喊道：
"我们在这里！我们在这里！我们在这里！我们在这里！"

The elephant smiled: "That was clear as a bell.
You kangaroos surely heard *that* very well."
"All I heard," snapped the big kangaroo, "was the breeze,
And the faint sound of wind through the far-distant trees.
I heard no small voices. And you didn't either."
And the young kangaroo in her pouch said, "Me, neither."

　　大象笑了："那声音像铃声一样清晰。这下，你们这两只袋鼠听到了吧。""我听到的只是风声，"袋鼠不耐烦地说，"那是穿过远处树林的微风。我没有听到什么细小的声音，你也没有。"她口袋里的小袋鼠跟着说："我也没听到。"

"Grab him!" they shouted. "And cage the big dope!
Lasso his stomach with ten miles of rope!
Tie the knots tight so he'll *never* shake loose!
Then dunk that dumb speck in the Beezle-Nut juice!"

"抓住他!"他们嚷道,"把这个大笨蛋关到笼子里去!用十米长的粗绳绑住他的肚子!打个死结,这样他就跑不掉了。然后把根本发不出声音的灰尘粒扔到滋滋冒着热气的坚果汤里!"

霍顿使尽全身力气拼命反抗。但是威克一伙人
多势众。他们打他，捶他，还准备把他拉到笼子里！
但是，他竭尽全力对镇长喊道："不要放弃！我完全
相信你们！一个人不管多么微小，他也是个人。如果
你们能让自己的声音被别人听到，你们这些小东西
就不会死！所以，加油吧，赶紧试一试！"

Horton fought back with great vigor and vim
But the Wickersham gang was too many for him.
They beat him! They mauled him! They started to haul
Him into his cage! But he managed to call
To the Mayor: "Don't give up! I believe in you all!
A person's a person, no matter how small!
And you very small persons will *not* have to die
If you make yourselves heard! *So come on, now, and TRY!*"

The Mayor grabbed a tom-tom. He started to smack it.
And, all over *Who*-ville, they whooped up a racket.
They rattled tin kettles! They beat on brass pans,
On garbage pail tops and old cranberry cans!
They blew on bazookas and blasted great toots
On clarinets, oom-pahs and boom-pahs and flutes!

镇长抓起一个手鼓,开始敲打。整个呼呼镇一片沸腾,他们敲打着锡壶、铜盘,还有垃圾桶盖和旧果酱罐!他们吹响火箭筒,用竖笛、长笛、单簧管、黑管,吹奏出巨大的嘟嘟声。

Great gusts of loud racket rang high through the air.
They rattled and shook the whole sky! And the Mayor
Called up through the howling mad hullabaloo:
"Hey, Horton! *How's this?* Is our sound coming through?"

　　狂风暴雨般的喧闹响彻云霄，惊天动地！镇长透过这疯狂的鼓噪声
大声呼喊："嗨！霍顿！这样行吗？听到我们的声音了吗？"

And Horton called back, "I can hear you just fine.
But the kangaroos' ears aren't as strong, quite, as mine.
They don't hear a thing! Are you *sure* all your boys
Are doing their best? Are they ALL making noise?
Are you sure every *Who* down in *Who*-ville is working?
Quick! Look through your town! Is there anyone shirking?"

　　霍顿回答:"我刚刚能听见。但是袋鼠的听力没有我的好。他们听不到!你确
定所有人都竭尽全力了吗?他们都在吆喝吗?你确定呼呼镇的每个人都在卖力吗?
快点儿!在镇子里好好找找!看看有没有人在偷懒?"

Through the town rushed the Mayor, from the east to the west.
But *every*one seemed to be doing his best.
*Every*one seemed to be yapping or yipping!
*Every*one seemed to be beeping or bipping!
But it *wasn't enough*, all this ruckus and roar!
He HAD to find someone to help him make more.
He raced through each building! He searched floor-to-floor!

　　镇长匆匆忙忙从镇子东头跑到西头。但是每个人似乎都在尽全力。每个人似乎都在声嘶力竭地喊啊，叫啊！每个人似乎都在扯破喉咙地吵啊，嚷啊！但是这样还不够！他必须找人来帮他弄出更大的动静。他在每幢楼里奔跑，一层一层地搜索。

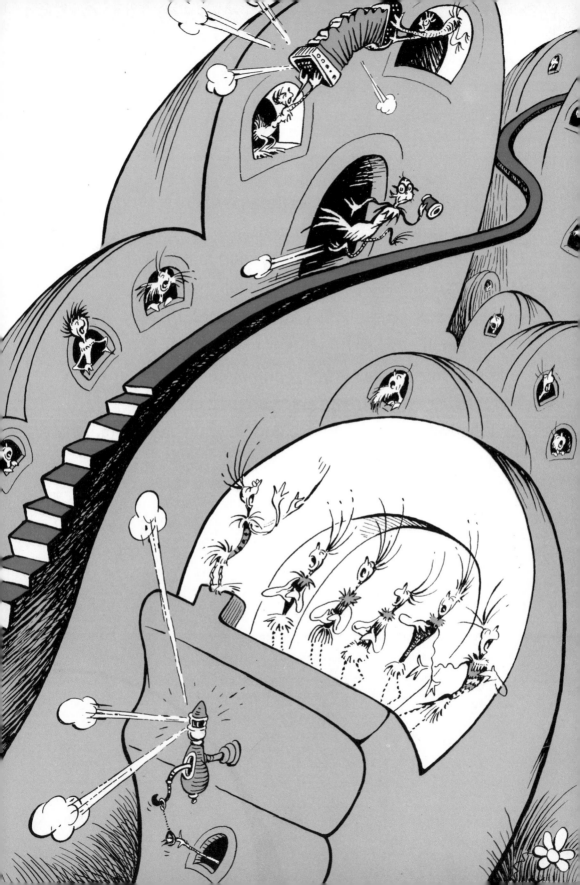

And, just as he felt he was getting nowhere,
And almost about to give up in despair,
He suddenly burst through a door and that Mayor
Discovered one shirker! Quite hidden away
In the Fairfax Apartments (Apartment 12-J)
A very small, *very* small shirker named Jo-Jo
Was standing, just standing, and bouncing a Yo-Yo!
Not making a sound! Not a yipp! Not a chirp!
And the Mayor rushed inside and he grabbed the young twerp!

　　正当他觉得无计可施，绝望得几乎想放弃的时候，镇长突然推开一扇门，发现了一个偷懒的人。这个家伙藏在费尔法公寓（12-J号公寓）里，他叫乔乔，这个小不点儿在开小差。他正站在那儿玩悠悠球呢！他没有发出一点儿声响！没有叫喊一声！镇长冲进来，抓住了这个小东西！

And he climbed with the lad up the Eiffelberg Tower.

"This," cried the Mayor, "is your town's darkest hour!
The time for all *Whos* who have blood that is red
To come to the aid of their country!" he said.
"We've GOT to make noises in greater amounts!
So, open your mouth, lad! For every voice counts!"

Thus he spoke as he climbed. When they got to the top,
The lad cleared his throat and he shouted out, "YOPP!"

　　他拉着小家伙往埃菲尔伯格塔爬去。"现在是我们镇最黑暗的时刻。"
镇长说,"是所有热血的呼呼保卫自己家园的时刻!"他说,"我们需要发出
最大的声音。所以,张开你的嘴,小伙子!每个声音都有一份力量!"

　　他一边爬一边说。当他们到达塔顶的时候,那个小家伙清了清喉咙,
大喊:"哟哦!"

And that Yopp . . .

That one small, extra Yopp put it over!

Finally, at last! From that speck on that clover

Their voices were heard! They rang out clear and clean.

And the elephant smiled. "Do you see what I mean? . . .

They've proved they ARE persons, no matter how small.

And their whole world was saved by the Smallest of All!"

"How true! Yes, how true," said the big kangaroo.

"And, from now on, you know what I'm planning to do? . . .

From now on, I'm going to protect them with you!"

And the young kangaroo in her pouch said, . . .

　　那声哟哦,那小小的一声哟哦加在了大家的叫喊声中!最后,他们的声音从苜蓿上的灰尘粒里传出来,终于被大家听到了。他们的声音清晰、纯净。大象笑了:"你们知道我的意思了吗?他们已经证明了不管多么微小,他们也是人。而且,他们中间最小的人拯救了他们的整个世界。"

　　"千真万确!没错,千真万确!"大袋鼠说,"从现在开始,你知道我打算怎么做吗?从现在开始,我要和你一起保护他们!"她口袋里的小袋鼠跟着说⋯⋯

"...ME, TOO!
From sun in the summer. From rain when it's fall-ish,
I'm going to protect them. No matter how small-ish!"

"我也一样！我要保护他们，使他们不受日晒雨淋之苦。我要保护他们，不管他们多么微小。"

阅读提示

　　苏斯博士的图画书《霍顿听见了呼呼的声音》讲述了一个令人感动的故事。感动之一源于它传达的生命平等和保护弱小的观念。无论多么微小，每个生命都有其生存权利，都应该受到尊重和保护。同样，无论多么微小，每个生命也都有存在的价值和意义，正是因为加入了乔乔——这个呼呼城最小的人的声音，呼呼们的叫喊才最终被大家听到。

　　感动之二在于霍顿守护小生命的那份执著。善良的大象霍顿相信生命是平等的，从他用鼻子小心翼翼地举起灰尘粒、把它放在柔软的苜蓿上的那一刻起，他就决定去守护灰尘粒上的小生命。他对呼呼镇的镇长说："别担心，我不会让你失望的。"于是，守护弱小生命的信念给了霍顿莫大的勇气，使他不怕大家的嘲笑甚至打骂，想尽一切办法证明呼呼们的存在；使他不顾伤痛和劳累，坚持寻找被抢走并丢弃的灰尘粒。从早上到中午，再到整个下午，在一望无际的苜蓿地里，霍顿就那样执著地搜索着、找寻着，当他终于在第三百万株苜蓿上听到呼呼的声音时，这只坚强的大象流泪了。

　　这个故事有一个温馨的结尾，那只曾经和妈妈一起嘲笑过霍顿的小袋鼠，最终也加入了守护呼呼的队伍，它用自己尚还稚嫩的小手，为这些生命撑起了一把明亮的小伞。

希望每个成人和孩子,在合上这本图画书的时候,在深深感动之余,也都能珍爱和保护周围的每一个生命,不管它多么微小。

儿童文学博士　苗　卉